This
Treasure Cove Story
belongs to

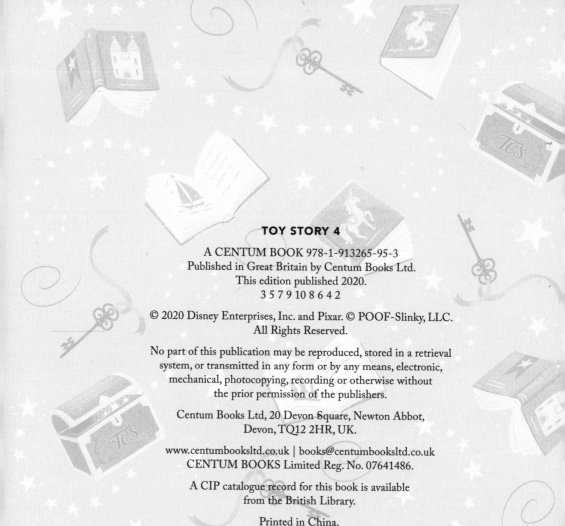

TOY STORY 4

A CENTUM BOOK 978-1-913265-95-3
Published in Great Britain by Centum Books Ltd.
This edition published 2020.
3 5 7 9 10 8 6 4 2

Centum Books Ltd, 20 Devon Square, Newton Abbot,
Devon, TQ12 2HR, UK.

www.centumbooksltd.co.uk | books@centumbooksltd.co.uk
CENTUM BOOKS Limited Reg. No. 07641486.

A CIP catalogue record for this book is available
from the British Library.

Printed in China.

centum

A Treasure Cove Story

Disney · PIXAR

TOY STORY 4

Adapted by
Josh Crute

Illustrated by
Matt Kaufenberg

Designed by
Tony Fejeran

Howdy, partner! Meet Woody, the sheriff round these parts. Woody loved his kid, Andy, and was the leader of the toys in Andy's room. But sometimes he needed help. Thankfully, his best friend, Bo Peep, was always there to lend a hand.

Then one day, **everything changed**.

Bo Peep was getting a new kid – and
Woody was **staying behind**.

Years later, Woody got a new kid, too. Her name was **Bonnie**. At **kindergarten orientation**, she was a little nervous.

Luckily, she had a sheriff around! When
a boy took her art supplies, Woody rustled
them up, along with some new ones. Bonnie
used her **imagination** to put them together
to make a new friend...

Forky!

To Woody's surprise, Forky **came to life**
– just like the other toys!

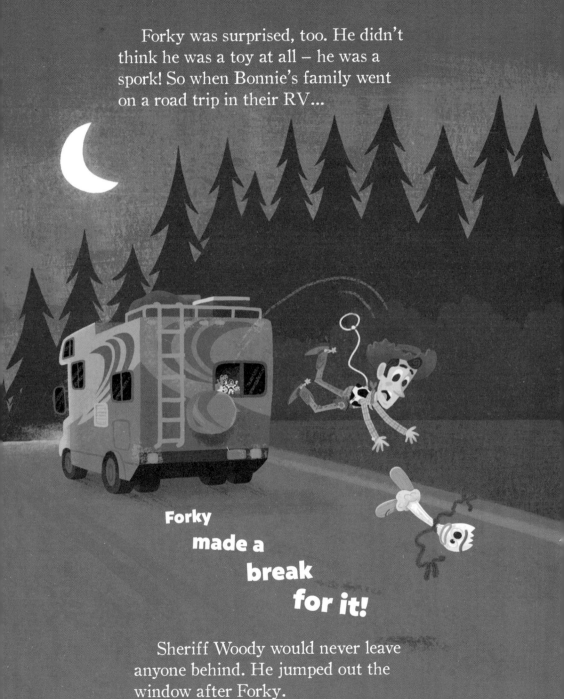

Forky was surprised, too. He didn't
think he was a toy at all – he was a
spork! So when Bonnie's family went
on a road trip in their RV...

Forky
made a
break
for it!

Sheriff Woody would never leave
anyone behind. He jumped out the
window after Forky.

Woody took Forky to the next town
to catch up with Bonnie. Then something
in the window of an antiques shop caught
his eye... **Bo's lamp!**

Woody and Forky went into the shop. Instead
of finding Bo, they saw a doll named **Gabby Gabby**.
She seemed friendly at first – but then she said
she wanted Woody's voice box. She told her team
to capture Woody and Forky!

Woody escaped to a nearby playground, where he saw a familiar face – **Bo Peep!** She and her tiny friend, **Giggle McDimples**, were travelling with a group of toys to find kids to play with. Bo said she would help Woody rescue Forky!

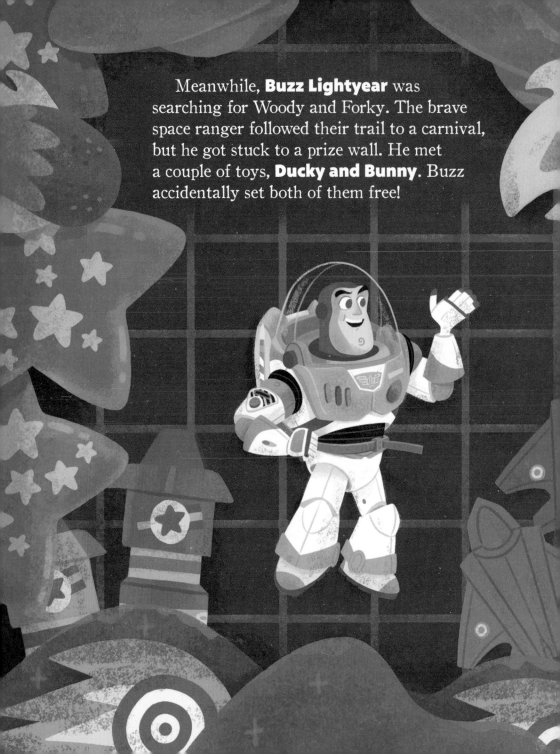

Meanwhile, **Buzz Lightyear** was searching for Woody and Forky. The brave space ranger followed their trail to a carnival, but he got stuck to a prize wall. He met a couple of toys, **Ducky and Bunny**. Buzz accidentally set both of them free!

Buzz found Woody and Bo, and the whole group sneaked into the antiques shop. Forky was trapped in a **tall cabinet**.

The shop's cat, **Dragon**, roamed the aisles, looking for stray toys to gobble up. The friends had to figure out a plan.

Bo found **Duke Caboom**, Canada's greatest stuntman. He would help rescue Forky, as well as Bo's sheep. They had been captured, too.

Duke leaped across the aisle to the cabinet. **But he didn't make it.** Dragon spotted him and the toys!

Bo found her sheep just as Dragon began to **chase** Duke. The toys held on tight!

They made it out of the shop – but Forky was still inside. Most of the group was too **tired and scared** to try a new plan. They decided to leave.

But Woody needed to get Forky. He made a deal with Gabby Gabby. In exchange for Forky, he gave her his **voice box**. And he would take her to Bonnie so she could have a kid, too.

The toys returned to help Woody and Gabby Gabby. But there was only **one way** to reach Bonnie. They went to the carnival and rode to the top of the Ferris wheel. Then they tied a long string around Duke's bike.

Duke took a deep breath, **revved his engine**...

...and **SOARED** over the crowd!

Thanks to Duke, the toys zipped across the carnival on the string. Then Gabby Gabby noticed a girl who was lost and needed a friend. Gabby Gabby was perfect for her! The girl hugged the doll close just before she found her parents. **Gabby Gabby got a kid!**

The toys found Bonnie. She was **thrilled**
to see Forky again!

Woody loved seeing
the two of them **so happy**.

And he was glad to be **reunited** with his friends.

Woody realised that lost and lonely toys
were everywhere, and he wanted to help them.
He knew with Bo and their friends, he could
accomplish anything!

Treasure Cove Stories

Please contact Centum Books to receive the full list of titles in the *Treasure Cove Stories* series. books@centumbooksltd.co.uk

*Book list may be subject to change. Not all titles are listed.